Lady Rample
and the Ghost
of Christmas Past

Lady Rample Mysteries – Book Five

Shéa MacLeod

Lady Rample and the Ghost of Christmas Past

Lady Rample Mysteries — Book Five

COPYRIGHT © 2018 by Shéa MacLeod

All rights reserved.

Printed in the United States of America.

Cover Art by Amanda Kelsey of Razzle Dazzle Designs

Editing by Alin Silverwood

Wishing you, dear reader, a very happy holiday season.

Chapter 1

"Penny for the Guy, Miss?"

I stared down at the small, slightly ragged child with some startlement. He'd a smudge of what I could only assume was soot across a chubby cheek. "Good gosh! Is it Bonfire Night already?" Where had the days gone?

Bonfire Night—or Guy Fawkes Night—was a celebration of Guy Fawkes's failure to blow up Parliament back in 1605. Children ran around with effigies, begging for money while the adults lit bonfires and fireworks and drank too much. It was a truly bizarre reason for a celebration, one which I didn't particularly understand. But any excuse for a cocktail, I always say!

"Yes, Miss." The child held out his metal bucket which already had at least a dozen coins. Behind him, two chums held what I could only assume was an effigy of Guy

Fawkes between them. It was a ghastly thing made of burlap stuffed with straw, a face painted on in boot black. Impatient, the child rattled his bucket. "Penny for the Guy?"

His angelic expression undid me. I'm not usually so soft, but what is one to do when a chubby-cheeked cherub begs one for a penny?

I fished around in my gray felt handbag until I found a copper and tossed it in his bucket. "There you go. Now get on with you."

The three children scampered off giggling, dragging their effigy behind them. A few stray wisps of straw scattered in their wake. I repressed a shudder—personally, I do not approve of Bonfire Night, though I do enjoy the food and drink that goes with it—and marched on.

It was early November—the fifth, to be precise—and the air had turned crisp with the autumnal chill of oncoming winter. A rusty oak leaf floated from a nearby branch and landed light as a feather on the pavement in front of me. Had it truly been less than a month since I'd been basking in the golden sun of the south of France?

I buttoned the top button of my claret merino wool coat. It was full length with the perfect sable collar, the height of fashion for the winter of 1932. I'd found it at Harrods shortly after my return to London and had to have it immediately. I refused to consider that my need for shopping was in any way connected with the loss of my paramour, Hale Davis. Ridiculous nonsense. I was an independent woman and not the sort to mourn the loss of any man.

Or so I told myself.

Speaking of Harrods, I was currently bound there on a mission to meet my aunt who had just returned from Paris. She'd rung me the previous night to inform me that she had a "Marvelous Idea." I repressed another shudder. Aunt Butty and her ideas were a dangerous combination.

My name is Ophelia, Lady Rample. I am not what you call "to the manor born," but rather married into it. My late husband Felix—God rest his soul—left me with a title and an enormous amount of wealth. For which I am forever grateful. It's amazing what one can get away with in life if one has money. It gave me a great deal of amusement to stick it in the faces of the aristocracy who liked to turn their collective noses up at anyone they deemed less than themselves. Which would be me, except I could probably buy most of them, so they let me be.

Harrods loomed ahead with its elaborate terra cotta facade. The Queen Anne Revival architecture was something to behold. And it ought to be. The royal family shopped there, though I'd never come across them. I imagine they had everything delivered. Personally, I like the hands-on approach to shopping.

Just before I passed through the doors, the blast of a motor horn startled me. Not that it was an unusual occurrence, even in the rarified air of Knightsbridge, but something tickled at my senses. Almost an impending sense of doom, I suppose. I turned and scanned the street, remembering with alarming clarity how I'd very nearly been run down on a similar street not that long ago. Fortunately, the police had captured the culprit with a little help from yours truly.

On the other side of Brompton Road stood a man dressed in an olive trench, battered fedora pulled low over his eyes. Though I couldn't see much of his face, there was something about his form, the way he stood, that jogged something far back in the recesses of my mind. I couldn't quite put my finger on it, but my unease grew.

Was he watching me?

Surely not. This was a busy street filled with people bustling about. One lone man standing several paces away meant nothing.

Turning purposefully, I nodded to the uniformed doorman and passed through to the inner sanctum. My low heels clicked against the marble floor as I made my way toward the escalator. As it worked its way upward, I found myself surrounded by marvelous Art Deco artwork in the Egyptian style. A bit over the top for my taste, but right up Aunt Butty's alley. I was surprised she hadn't turned her flat's sitting room into an Egyptian temple.

The escalator arrived eventually at the fourth floor, spilling out onto a wide marble foyer directly opposite the tea room which was situated under a massive stained-glass window set in the ceiling. A string quartet played a soothing number while diners nibbled on tea cakes and murmured in appropriately low voices.

"Ophelia!" A buxom woman with waved, gray hair and a garishly orange cloche hat from a decade ago half stood and waved wildly, her ample bosoms nearly diving into her tea. "Yoo-hoo! Over here!"

The maître d' flushed crimson as he scampered to my side. I couldn't tell if it was from embarrassment or anger. Frankly it could go either way. Aunt Butty had that effect on people.

"I see my aunt," I murmured softly to him, as he helped me out of my overcoat. "I'll just make my way over."

The maître d' sketched a bow, his pencil moustache twitching ever so slightly. He seemed most grateful as he hurried off to hang up my coat.

I made my way between the tables toward Aunt Butty. I was dying for a cup of tea and a biscuit. Who was I kidding? Half a dozen biscuits.

I barely had time to sit down before Aunt Butty was upon me. "Ophelia, I have had the most Marvelous Idea." She gazed at me expectantly.

"So you said." A waiter leapt to help me into my seat.

"Christmas."

I lifted an eyebrow. "What about it?" I went about pouring my tea and helping myself to a handful of biscuits from the tiered tray. It appeared there were spiced ones and lemon ones. Lemon were my favorite, but spice would do just as well in a pinch. If only there were chocolate.

As if reading my mind, the waiter disappeared, only to reappear with a second tea tier loaded with chocolate biscuits, scones, and little cakes covered in icing. Glorious!

"I fancy a proper old-fashioned English Christmas this year," Aunt Butty informed me as we tucked into our treats. "You know the sort. Cozy cottage in the countryside. Smoke curling from the chimney. A proper Christmas tree and all the trimmings…"

"Yes, yes. I know what a proper Christmas looks like." I had, after all, grown up in the tiny country village of Chipping Poggs. Proper English country Christmases abounded in my youth. That didn't mean I enjoyed them. "What's the point?"

"The point is, I have rented a cottage." She beamed at me as if she'd just done something spectacular.

"A cottage?" It wasn't exactly Aunt Butty's style. She was more likely to take over Buckingham Palace than a small cottage in the middle of nowhere. "Where exactly have you taken this cottage?"

Her smile grew wider. "In this marvelous little village called Sheepswick Hill. Doesn't it sound delightful?"

"Delightful." I set down my tea cup with a clatter. "Where precisely is this village located?"

"It's in the Cotswolds," she admitted. "But it's nowhere near Chipping Poggs. I assure you. I have it all planned. Mr. Singh has his marching orders. You will be there."

I sighed and took a fortifying bite of lemon biscuit. "You know how I feel about the country." And the Cotswolds in particular.

She sipped her tea beatifically. "Yes, I know. And it's high time to put that to rest. You will be at Christmas at Sheepswick Hill at my rented cottage and we shall have the most marvelous country Christmas ever." She said it was such finality as if she would pull it from the very ether.

I took a sip of my own tea, wishing it was something very much stronger. "And what if I say no?"

I'd no idea her smile could get any slyer, but somehow, she managed it. "Oh, you won't. For someone special is going to be there."

I felt a little quiver of anticipation. Had she managed to talk Hale into joining us? Surely not. By now he was married and probably a father. There was no way that Hale Davis would be there for Christmas. Which meant that I didn't feel much like celebrating this year.

"I'm afraid I'll be busy, Aunt." Surely, I could come up with something to do. At the very least, I could enjoy a bit of quiet time at home. I shuddered at the thought.

"I'll cut you out of my will."

I snorted. "I don't need your money."

"I shall never speak to you again."

"Hardly likely."

Her jaw hardened. "You will go because I want you to."

"No," I said stubbornly.

"Please, Ophelia," she wheedled. "It would mean the world to me." She placed the back of her hand dramatically against her forehead. "I'm getting on in years, you know. Who knows how many Christmases I have left."

I rolled my eyes. "You're stubborn enough to outlive us all. Fine. I'll be there."

"Delightful!" She clapped her hands, advanced age forgotten. "Let's plan the menu."

"I don't care what we have as long as there's Christmas pudding and booze."

Aunt Butty pulled a piece of paper and pencil nub from her handbag, perched a pair of reading glasses on the end of her nose, and scrawled "Booze" across the top of the paper.

I took another biscuit. This was going to be a long afternoon.

That night was the Pennyfather's party. Louise Pennyfather was my aunt's dearest friend, and every year she and her husband threw a big soiree for Bonfire Night. Fancy dress, cocktails, dancing, the complete works.

Naturally I was invited, as was my best friend, Charles "Chaz" Raynott. Apparently, Louise had forgiven us for getting her involved in a somewhat murderous mystery—and the kidnapping of her beloved dog, Peaches—on the French Riviera.

Chaz picked me up in his new sports car, a slinky, black Invicta four-seater. He was dressed all in black from head to toe but more than 100 years out-of-date in Regency formalwear, complete with greatcoat which billowed behind him in proper Mr. Darcy fashion.

"Whatever are you supposed to be?" I asked, eyeing him up and down.

"Beau Brummel, darling," he said. "Who else?"

Who else, indeed. Naturally Chaz would choose the most celebrated arbiter of men's fashion. Historically speaking, of course.

Chaz Raynott was not only my best friend, but also my sounding board and partner in crime. In fact, he would've made an excellent second husband except for the small problem of my being the wrong gender. A secret I kept close to my chest. After all, it was illegal. Which I thought nonsense, but there wasn't much I could do about that, society being what it was.

"Smashing gown, old thing," he said, giving me the once over. "Take it out of mothballs?"

I laughed. "I got it out of Aunt Butty's closet. Had to take in a few nips and tucks." Not as many as I would've liked. I was a couple inches taller and a few pounds lighter than my aunt, but our figures were overwhelmingly similar. With curves in all the wrong places for the current fashion.

The particular gown I'd liberated from Aunt Butty's closet was from sometime in the Edwardian era. It was the precise shade and color of a pumpkin. I paired it with long strands of jet beads and a matching jet masquerade mask. I suppose I could've gone all out and bought a proper costume. But why do that when I could simply rummage in Aunt Butty's wardrobe? I swear the woman never threw anything away.

Inside the elegant Georgian townhouse, a crush of the upper crust wandered from room to room, clutching cocktails and *vol-au-vent*, no doubt prepared by Louise's French cook. The party goers had gone all out on their costumes with everything from Little Bo Peep complete with a live sheep to a frightening-looking mummy trailing bandage tails behind him.

Louise Pennyfather herself greeted me with a tray of cocktails. She was wearing a rather garish Egyptian costume which did not particularly show off her gaunt frame to advantage. Based on the black wig, eyes rimmed in kohl, and elaborate gold headpiece, I assumed she was Cleopatra.

"Try this, Ophelia," she said, thrusting a cocktail glass in my direction. "It's a Corpse Reviver #2. Found it in an American cocktail book my husband brought back from his travels. Tell me what you think."

I took a sip. It was surprisingly delicious, but not as sweet as I would have expected. "It would be better without the absinthe," I admitted.

She sighed. "So I told Mr. Pennyfather, but he insisted on mixing exactly as ordered. The man has no sense of adventure. Go on and enjoy the party."

As we strolled through the crush, I linked arms with Chaz. "What are you doing for Christmas?"

He took a sip of his cocktail. "I imagine I'll have dinner at the club or some such." He wasn't particularly close to his family, for obvious reasons.

"Why don't you join Aunt Butty and me? She insists on renting a cottage out in some ghastly village and having a proper, old fashioned Christmas. You *must* come."

"Misery loves company?"

I grinned. "You know me so well."

"Very well. If I must." But I could tell he was thrilled to be invited.

The rest of the evening passed quickly. There was dancing, a ridiculous apple bob in which Aunt Butty nearly drowned herself trying to win and, as the herd thinned, a game of charades. I escaped out onto the terrace to enjoy a bit of the fresh night air.

As I sipped at cocktail number three—or was it four?—I stared up at the nearly full moon. A rustling caught my ear and I glanced toward the bushes that marked the property line between the Pennyfather's back garden and their neighbor's. My heart rate kicked up as I remembered the man outside Harrods. Was he here? Spying on me?

I told myself not to be ridiculous. There was no way he could know I was at this party. And while I may have found him vaguely familiar, he was likely just another of many faces in the crowd.

But as the moon slid behind a cloud and the shadows grew thick, I hurried back inside. No use tempting fate.

Chapter 2

The road to Shipswick Hill wound around the gently rolling hills of the Cotswolds, through chocolate box villages, and past neat little farms. Hemmed in by hedgerows that nearly blocked the light of the weak winter sun, the road was barely wide enough for my cobalt blue **Mercedes 710 SSK Roadster.**

Once upon a time, this gorgeous countryside had been my home, but my own life had not been so beautiful. While most of the vicars of the Church of England were happy enough to imbibe at the local pub, enjoy the odd game of darts, and ignore their parishioners' less-than-holy pursuits, my father was not cut from the same cloth. The vicar of Chipping Poggs was the sort of man who insisted on obedience at all costs, church before child, uncooperative daughters locked in attics, that sort of thing.

Until Aunt Butty had rescued me at the age of sixteen, my life had been a misery. Why would she force me back here? For while we were miles from my home village and unlikely to meet anyone we knew, the very fields stirred unpleasant memories.

The road before me rose a bit before turning downhill ever so slightly. Below me, the village of Sheepswick Hill spread out like something from a picture postcard. Thatched roof houses, thick stone walls, the church spire rising from the trees. A low mist blanketed everything in a soft haze. Frost still tipped the grass and coated fence posts. It was, in a word, perfect.

I passed the pub on my left, still closed at this hour of the morning. As were the greengrocers next door and the butchers next to that. A black-cloaked figure stood in front of the church door and for a moment my heart fluttered even though I knew that figure wasn't my father. He was plumper and a little more stooped about the shoulders.

I roared past, exiting the village, headed further out into the countryside. I frowned. Aunt Butty had said she'd rented a cottage in Sheepswick Hill, but I had left the village in my rearview mirror.

A short way out of the village, I noticed another figure walking along the roadside. I stiffened, recognizing the olive trench and battered fedora. Surely, the man I'd seen outside Harrod's couldn't possibly be in the Cotswolds. I must be imagining things. But as I roared past, I caught a glimpse of his face and was certain it was the same man. Why was he here?

I told myself it must be a coincidence. It was nearly Christmas. He was probably just visiting family. But I wasn't certain I believed it.

At precisely the point in which I was to turn loomed a pair of wrought iron gates standing open, partially covered in ivy. A neat little plaque pronounced this to be Sheepswick Hall.

"Aunt Butty, you sly minx," I murmured.

I wound down the drive through a tunnel of trees which turned daylight to near twilight. As I burst from the trees, above me towered a grand manner in the Tudor style. Diamond paned windows and dark wood beams did give the place a bit of a cottage feel, for all its monstrosity, but that was where the semblance ended.

I grinned as I screeched to a halt in a cloud of dust from the gravel drive. Country cottage indeed. Aunt Butty had only gone and rented what was likely the grandest manner house in the whole of the village.

Before I could pour myself from the motorcar, the front door swung open and Mr. Singh, Aunt Butty's butler, appeared. He opened my door with a flourish and bowed elegantly.

"Welcome, My Lady." His tone was smooth and melodious, carrying exotic hints of the land from which he'd come. Today's *dastar* was lavender to match the sash about his waist. The rest of him was dressed just as a proper English butler should be, in a crisp white shirt and gloves and black suit.

"Thank you, Mr. Singh," I said, taking his hand. As he helped me from the car, a small urchin screeched up from nowhere and began rummaging around in the boot. "I say, who is that?"

"His name is Bobby. His aunt works at the pub. Your aunt thought he was… adorable. So she hired him to assist with luggage today." Mr. Singh's expression was stoic, giving away nothing of his thoughts on the matter. As far as Mr. Singh was concerned, whatever Aunt Butty wanted, Aunt Butty got.

"So I see. My aunt about?"

"The sitting room, My Lady. I'd show you but…"

"Don't be daft man." I waved him off. "You'd better supervise the boy lest my luggage find itself tumbled down the hill."

I strode inside to find the foyer kitted out with hanging banners, guarded by suits of armor polished to a high shine. The only nod to anything feminine or festive was a vase of white hot-house roses on the oak table gracing the middle of the entry.

Down the hall on the right, I found the sitting room with its appropriately low ceiling crossed with beams, a delightful nook with a roaring fire, and a record player whirling away in the corner playing something Christmasy. It sounded like *The Star of Bethlehem,* perhaps.

"Hello, Aunt Butty," I said, stripping off my gloves as I sauntered into the sitting room.

Aunt Butty was standing at the bar, whipping up some concoction or other. "Ophelia, you've made it. Would you like a cocktail? I'm experimenting. This one's called a Seventh Heaven. Doesn't it sound delightful?"

"Don't mind if I do." I would've preferred a highball or perhaps an Aviation. But whatever a Seventh Heaven was, it would have to do. I suppose it would get me in the Christmas spirit — which was lacking at the moment.

"I see you haven't got any decorations up yet." After divesting myself of my coat, I took a seat on the couch.

"Oh, no," Aunt Butty said, taking a sip of her pale pink concoction. "I was waiting for you. We're going to do it together." She gave a nod of approval and poured the liquid into a second martini glass.

I groaned softly. "If I knew you were going to put me to work, I would have brought my maid down with me."

"Speaking of Maddie, where is she?"

"I sent her home to celebrate the holidays with her parents," I said.

"They're Jews. They don't celebrate Christmas," she pointed out as she handed me my pink cocktail.

"No, of course not, but I do. It will give her a nice chance to be home with her family, and I can do for myself for a couple of weeks. Besides, Hanukkah starts on Christmas Eve this year." I was, after all, used to doing for myself. I'd been doing it since I was a small child. Having a lady's maid was a fairly new experience for me.

"I imagine I should've offered my maid the same," Aunt Butty mused. "But frankly, I needed her help."

"Help? That girl is a menace," I said. "She's more likely to cause extra work."

"True, but she will never be trained properly if she doesn't have experience."

I said nothing. Some people simply aren't cut out for service. And Aunt Butty's maid was one of those people.

I took a sip of the Seventh Heaven. It was surprisingly sweet and tasted…pink. There was no other word for it. Not to mention Aunt Butty had broken out the good gin. I approved.

"Hello, darlings. A cocktail for me?" Chaz strode into the room, hands shoved in his pockets.

"When did you get here, darling?" I asked.

"Ridiculously early, old thing. You were likely still abed."

Aunt Butty waved him toward the drinks cart as she went to sit down near the fire. "Help yourself. There's some left in the shaker. I can't be bothered." Never one to mince words, my aunt

Chuckling, Chaz helped himself to libations. "So what's on the agenda? Have any parties planned? Exotic dinners? Gorgeous guests?" He waggled his eyebrows.

Aunt Butty laughed. "None of that I'm afraid. What I want is a genuinely old-fashioned English Christmas. Complete with Yule log and wassail."

"How dull," Chaz said as he strolled to the window. I didn't know what he would see. It was nearly dark outside. The sun set so early these days. "Oh, I say, I think there's somebody skulking about on the grounds."

"Really? Where?" I set down my cocktail, jumped up from the sofa, and hurried to the window. Peering out, I could see a faint light bobbing its way through the bushes, appearing and disappearing at will. Almost as if it were carried by one of the fairy folk. "Someone is spying on us! Maybe it's that man that's been following me."

"Don't be ridiculous, darling," Aunt Butty said, having not moved from her perch. "There's a public footpath that goes through there. I'm sure it's just a local taking a stroll."

"After dark?" I asked.

"Oh, you know how these country people are," Aunt Butty said. "They're made of sterner stuff than us city folk. A nighttime jaunt is nothing to the likes of them."

"What I want to know is what's this spy business? Didn't you get enough of that in Devon?" Chaz asked.

Chaz was, of course, referring to my previous shenanigans at a house party in Devon over the summer. While there, we'd found ourselves up to our veritable eyeballs in spies and murder.

"Oh, nothing so outrageous as all of that," I assured him. "It's all just rather odd." I quickly told him about my having seen the man staring at me outside Harrods and then later seeing the same man in the village.

"That is odd," Chaz agreed. "But it could be just a coincidence."

"That's what I told her," Aunt Butty said, waving her cocktail around. Thank goodness it was nearly empty, or she'd have been wearing half of it. "But you know how Ophelia is. She likes to make mountains of molehills."

"I do not," I said, affronted. "And I don't believe in coincidences. What would that man at Harrods be doing in a village like Sheepswick Hill?"

"Well, *you* were outside Harrods and now you're in Sheepswick Hill," Chaz pointed out with maddening logic.

"Well, I have a reason to be here," I insisted.

"Maybe he does, too," Aunt Butty said. She held out her glass to Chaz. "Be a dear and get me a refill, will you?"

"But of course, Butty darling," he said with a little bow. While he busied himself fixing my aunt a new cocktail, I remained at the window, peering out into the darkness.

The light continued on its way, growing dimmer as it moved behind trees and shrubbery until it disappeared altogether. Perhaps Aunt Butty was right. It was simply a local out for a stroll along the footpath. Perhaps someone on their way home, coming from the pub. Or maybe my imagination really was getting away with me. I returned to the sofa, tossed back the last of my cocktail, and strolled over to Chaz.

"Wouldn't mind a refill myself," I said, holding it out to him.

He gave me a smile. "You know we're only teasing you," he said soothingly. "But I really do think it's just a coincidence. Nothing to worry about, darling. These things happen."

"I hope you're right."

"Let's say for a moment some fellow really is following you," he mused as he mixed up my drink, following Aunt Butty's careful instructions. "You said you didn't recognize him."

"That's right."

"Then why would he have any reason to be following you?" He held out my glass.

I shrugged as I took the proffered drink. I took a sip. Much better than Aunt Butty's version, though I'd never tell her that. Sweeter and stronger. "I have no idea," I admitted. "I just think it's very strange to have seen the same person in two places. And he seemed so familiar. Though I haven't been able to place him. It'll come to me eventually."

"Well, perhaps when it does that will solve the mystery."

"I suppose." But I wasn't convinced. There was something about that man. Something about the way he looked at me. It just didn't sit easy.

I was determined to enjoy the rest of the evening and ignore my better instincts, but no matter what I did, I still remained uneasy. Like that feeling you get before a storm breaks. Something was coming, and it didn't bode well.

The next day arrived with a flash of pink across the sky, the air crisp and cold. The edges of the window were framed in frost and, as my breath puffed against the panes, the glass fogged over. Outside the sky was bright and cloudless with that hard edge of light that comes only with winter.

My room had a good view of the back garden, currently bedded down for the cold. A layer of frost coated every branch and bramble, giving it an almost fairytale appearance.

Shivering a bit in the chill air, I quickly dressed in a plain gray wool dress with little pearl buttons up the font and slid my feet into a pair of plain black pumps. Without Maddie to help me, I put my hair up in a simple twist and added a quick layer of powder to my face along with a swipe of pale pink lipstick. Then I made my way quickly to the breakfast room.

Aunt Butty had brought her cook along and the woman had worked a miracle in the kitchen. Laid out upon the buffet were kedgeree, fresh-made crumpets dripping in butter, homemade marmalade and strawberry preserves, eggs, bacon, sausages, black pudding, grilled mushrooms and tomatoes, and a pot of baked beans. It was enough to make my mouth water!

Ignoring the tea, I poured myself a cup of coffee from the silver urn, helped myself to some breakfast, and seated myself at the table. I was alone, the only sound the ticking of the grandfather clock in the hallway. In the silence, I could almost imagine I heard the patter of tiny hooves on the rooftop. I smiled at the thought.

Apparently, Aunt Butty was still abed. I wondered if Chaz was, too. Although knowing him, he could be out and about already, looking for his latest conquest. Though where he'd find one in the middle of nowhere was beyond me.

Mr. Singh appeared in the doorway, gave me a slight bow, and announced, "My lady, your guest has arrived."

I stared at him over the rim of my coffee cup. "My guest?"

"Lord Rample," he supplied.

"Lord Rample?" For a moment, my heart stilled, before remembering it couldn't, of course, be my husband, seeing as how Felix was quite dead and had been for well over a year now. Mr. Singh must be referring to my husband's cousin, Alphonse, who'd inherited the title, the money pit of a manor, and not much else. I, however, never referred to him by his title. To me, he was Binky. Bucktooth Binky behind his back. "I didn't invite him."

"Your Aunt Butty did," Mr. Singh said as Binky bumbled into the room, nearly knocking over a figurine gracing a marble-topped side table.

Binky blinked at the offending table before turning to me. "Are you not happy to see me, cousin?" He tried for an innocent look but failed miserably.

There was a loaded question if I ever heard one. "I'm not your cousin, Binky."

Mr. Singh bowed, murmured his apologies, and exited from the room. His footsteps echoed down the hall, each step leisurely yet precise.

"Close enough." Binky strolled over to the sideboard and began piling his plate high. He looked thinner than when last I saw him. Which had the unfortunate side effect of making him look more like a beaver than ever. I would have expected the opposite, beavers being fluffy little creatures, but the gauntness made his prominent front teeth stand out more than ever.

"I am glad you could join us for the holidays," I said, not sure it was true. Binky could be... contentious. I was going to have words with my aunt, as I was certain she had something to do with his appearance at this house party.

"Oh, there you are, Binky." Aunt Butty said, sailing into the room in a day dress of shocking green. "I'm glad to see you made it in one piece. You must have left the wilds of Yorkshire at a ridiculously early hour."

"I'm an early riser, as you know," Binky said, helping himself to a cup of coffee. I held back a snort as he sat down across from me. Binky was a lazy lay about. "But in actuality," he continued. "I left yesterday. Stayed overnight with a friend near Loughborough."

I was amazed Binky had any friends, but I wisely kept my mouth shut.

"I wonder if the other guest has arrived yet," Aunt Butty said aloud, as she piled her plate high with food.

"Other guest?" I stopped with my fork halfway to my mouth, a quiver of excitement hitting me in the stomach. *Could it be?* A bit of egg slid off and splatted against the edge of the plate before plopping onto the tablecloth, leaving a yellow mark.

"Why yes. I invited—"

Before she could finish her sentence, there was a great fuss in the hallway. Mr. Singh appeared once again in the doorway. "Miss Farthing," he announced. His expression, as usual, was unfathomable, but there was something in his eyes that looked a little pinched. Who could disturb the unflappable Mr. Singh to such a degree?

Aunt Butty clapped her hands together and jumped up from the table. "At last!"

"Who the deuce is Miss Farthing?" I muttered to myself.

Binky stood politely as the new arrival sailed into the room. The stranger was a woman of about my own age, but fashionably thin where I was overtly curvy. She had an annoyingly pert nose, perfectly coiffed hair, impossibly bright lipstick, and a haughty and superior attitude that told the world she thought she was better than everyone else. I disliked her immediately.

"Ophelia," Aunt Butty said, "meet Olivia Farthing. Your cousin."

Chapter 3

"My *cousin*?" I could only stare, gobsmacked. I knew there were cousins of some sort or other on my father's side, but we'd had nothing to do with any of them when I was growing up. I certainly didn't remember one called Olivia Farthing. And since Aunt Butty was my mother's only sibling and sans children, I knew I'd no cousins on that side of the family. "How?"

It was, perhaps, a rather daft thing to say, but it certainly didn't call for Olivia's braying laugh. "I dunno. Second cousins? Twice removed? Can never get these things straight. Now who is *this*?" She sashayed over to Binky, a mercenary gleam in her eyes.

"Lord Rample," I supplied, using his title for perhaps the first time ever. "Aunt?"

"Her father and my mother were siblings. Olivia is technically *my* cousin. Mine and your mothers'. By Uncle Harold's second wife."

Well, that explained the age discrepancy, I suppose. Uncle Harold, my maternal grandmother's brother, had been dead for yonks. In fact, I only vaguely remembered meeting him as a small child. He'd seemed impossibly old and smelled of cigar smoke and whiskey. He talked in a loud voice and disliked children immensely. That had been clear. I'd been locked into my room for the entirety of his visit.

Olivia was busy fawning over Binky, who appeared horrified. Which amused me no end. Apparently, Olivia hadn't got the memo that Binky was broke.

"Join us for breakfast, Olivia," Aunt Butty ordered. "We were about to discuss our plans."

"Plans for what, cousin?" Olivia flounced into a seat, pouting because she couldn't sit next to Binky who'd sat on my other side as far away from her as he could get. For his part, Binky seemed relieved.

"The holiday, of course," Aunt Butty said as if Olivia had taken leave of her senses. "We must decorate. And plan for the party."

"Party?" This was the first I'd heard of it. Aunt Butty had told Chaz the holidays were to be a quiet affair.

"I told you, Ophelia."

"No, you didn't, Aunt." I gave her a stern look. "What party?"

"A Christmas Eve party. We shall invite the entire village."

I choked on a bite of crumpet.

"What a marvelous idea!" Olivia clapped her hands together. "I shall help. I'm a whiz at organizing."

"I just bet you are," I mumbled.

"What's that?" She blinked innocently at me, but there was a cold shrewdness beneath the facade. There and gone so fast I might have missed it if I hadn't been eyeing her so closely.

I gave her my own innocent look. "I said, what's the plan, Aunt Butty?" I was starting to feel a bit of excitement for my aunt's planned festivities. Aunt Butty threw the best parties, and Christmas did have a certain magic to it.

Over breakfast, my aunt outlined her plans for decorating the house, throwing the greatest party the Cotswolds had ever seen, and the Christmas Day family feast. She finished up with, "I invited your parents."

I choked again. This time on bacon. All excitement fled. "*Why* would you do *that*?"

"They *are* family, as unfortunate as it may be. Don't worry. My invitation was declined." She seemed neither bothered nor surprised.

I swallowed, relieved, and snagged another piece of bacon.

Just then Chaz strolled in, and Olivia's eyes lit up. Aunt Butty quickly made introductions while Olivia fluttered her lashes and thrust out her rather flat bosom. I almost laughed out loud. She was entirely beating up the wrong tree.

"Hullo, all. How's things? Good to see you Binky." Chaz grabbed a crumpet and lounged in the chair on my other side, much to Olivia's frustration. "Singh says you got some things planned for the holidays, Butty. Anything I can do?"

"Help Ophelia select a Christmas tree," she said promptly. "I've already spoken to the groundskeeper, and he's agreed to go with you to cut it down. And make sure he gives you plenty of greenery. I want every mantle and balustrade covered in holly, fir, and ribbons. I wonder if there's any mistletoe on the property?"

"If there is, we'll find it," Chaz assured her, giving me a wink.

Olivia went red in the face. "Why should they get all the fun? I want to look for a tree." She clearly didn't, but she also clearly didn't want me alone with Chaz.

The almost made me laugh out loud. How delightful would it be to let the nasty Olivia fawn over Chaz to no avail! Perhaps the devil made me do it, but I decided to nudge things along. Just because Olivia was such a pill. Not to mention and obvious gold-digger.

"You can go with Chaz," I offered.

Her face brightened.

"And I'll stay here with Binky to start preparations for the party." I wondered if my expression was as wicked as I felt. She was clearly torn between which man to go after. Chaz was the handsomer of the two by far, but Binky had a title.

Her face fell, and her eyes snapped angrily. Clearly uncertain what to do, she was stuck. One way or the other, she'd either have to leave me alone with one of the men or share one with me. And she very clearly did not like either option.

"Olivia, I could use you here," Aunt Butty said, putting an end to it. "We will need to prepare invitations."

Olivia opened her mouth to protest, but Aunt Butty was already off on another tangent. "Binky, do you suppose you could check out the attic? See what they have in the way of decorations?"

The image of the fastidious and mincing Binky poking about a spiderweb-festooned attic space made me grin. He shot me a look.

"Of course, Lady Lucas." But he looked miserable.

She tittered. "How many times have I told you to call me Butty? We're practically related, more's the pity. Now this is what I'm thinking…"

I zoned out as Aunt Butty rambled on about cakes, musicians, dances, and such. I had really hoped that this year I'd be celebrating the holidays with Hale Davis, my former paramour. Things had been going well between us, or so I thought, until a past fling informed him she was pregnant with his child.

Being the sort of man he was, he insisted on taking care of the child and the woman. And knowing what sort of man he was, I hadn't tried to stop him. It wouldn't be right. A child deserved a good father.

I had no desire to remarry, but that didn't mean that part of me didn't long for love and companionship. Something I'd thought I'd found with Hale. The thought of him living my dreams with another woman made me ache deep inside. I shoved it down and ignored it. No use crying over spilled milk. Water under the bridge and all that.

I was only relieved to be out of London, so I wouldn't accidentally run into him. Unlikely, since we swam in vastly different circles, but the thought was always there, nagging away at the back of my mind. Many a time I'd rounded a corner and thought I saw him there, only to discover a stranger. I pushed all thoughts of Hale from my mind, determined to enjoy the present.

"Ready, Ophelia?" Chaz interrupted my thoughts.

"What?"

"Christmas tree hunting," he prodded.

"Oh, yes, of course. Just let me change into something more practical."

As I left the room, my newly found cousin stared daggers at me. I tried to dredge up my former amusement, but the cheeriness of the morning had gone out.

I didn't want to ruin any of my couture clothing, and since my wardrobe didn't run to mucking about items, I asked Mr. Singh to dig me something up. He managed to find a surprisingly well-fitting pair of overalls and a rather baggy checkered overcoat. Naturally, as country houses often do, there was a vast assortment of Wellies from which to choose. I found a pair that fit me well enough and joined Chaz and the groundsman outside.

"Let's go find a Christmas tree." I was determined to rediscover the joy of the season.

"This is Mr. Phelps, old thing," Chaz said by way of introduction. He was dressed in the height of fashion—high waisted woolen trousers and a perfectly tailored navy peacoat which made his broad shoulders appear broader and his narrow waist slimmer.

"Jes' call me Phelps. Don't hold with formalities 'roun' here." The groundsman tugged on his beat-up cap.

Phelps was the epitome of a man of the country. Although in his sixties with a slight stoop to his shoulders and a bit of thickening in the waist, he was still powerfully built and surprisingly spry. He had the well-weathered features of someone who spent a lot of time out of doors and carried a shotgun in his rough worn hands—just in case, he said. I wasn't sure if the "just in case" was because we might be set upon by highwaymen, or because he wanted rabbit stew for dinner.

He led the way through the gardens and out into the fields, striding along at such a pace I was quickly winded. Chaz, on the other hand, had no trouble keeping up. Likely his longer legs. At least that's what I told myself.

At last we came to the woods edging the property and plunged into the eternal gloom. Initially it was all alders and poplars and oaks and whatnot, but soon firs began to sprout up between the rest until it was nearly all evergreens in neat little rows. Clearly, they'd been planted there rather than growing naturally.

"Whatcha think o' this 'un?" Phelps asked, coming to a stop in front of a rather spindly looking tree. It was a nice enough height, but the back half was somewhat... sparse.

"Oh, I think we can do better, don't you, Ophelia?" Chaz said.

"Indubitably," I managed, somewhat breathlessly. I had developed a stitch in my side.

Phelps let out a sound that was halfway between a grunt and a snort and marched on, deeper into the wood.

"'Ow 'bout this?"

This time, the tree was much fuller with all its branches, but alas, it wasn't even as tall as I was. I doubted Aunt Butty would be pleased.

"Taller, I think, old chap," Chaz said, since I was currently speechless. He thrust a flask at me and I took a deep swallow, almost choking when I realized it was whiskey and not water. Naturally, I took another swallow.

We walked on, stopping here and there to inspect various offerings, none of which appealed. Until at last we found the very thing. It had to be at least ten foot tall! And marvelously fluffy with good, thick branches just right for hanging ornaments.

"Perfect!" I announced.

Phelps lifted his cap to reveal a balding head and gave himself a good scratch before settling the cap. "Gonna need more'n me to haul it out." His tone was morose.

"That's alright, then," I assured him. "You can have the gardener, or someone, help. Or Chaz."

"Don't volunteer me, love." He turned back to Phelps. "I'll send someone out if you like."

"They'll never find their way back 'ere," Phelps said. I'll go an' get 'em."

So after marking the tree with a red kerchief, the three of us made our way back to the manor house. We were at the very edge of the wood when I noticed something out of the corner of my eye. A shadow, fliting from tree to tree, following us while trying to stay out of sight.

"Don't look now, but someone is following us," I hissed so only Chaz could hear.

"Let me have a look see," he whispered back.

I kept pace with Phelps, while Chaz dropped behind making a show of needing to retie the laces on his boot. Once he'd fiddled a bit, he straightened up and broke into a jog to catch up.

"Well?" I whispered.

"You're not wrong."

"How are we going to catch him?"

He lifted a brow. "Are you sure we should?"

"Of course, we should!" My voice had grown a little loud and Phelps glanced back. In a lower tone I said, "We need to find out why he's following us."

Chaz gestured toward our guide. "You go on. Chat to Phelps. Draw attention."

"What will you be doing?"

"Chasing down our creeper."

With a nod, I hurried to catch up to Phelps and proceeded to chatter at him loudly and inanely. I asked him copious questions about his work, how long he'd been at the manor, and so on. To which I received monosyllabic grunts. It didn't put me off one bit. I only got louder.

"What'cher yellin' for?" he finally asked. "'ard o' 'earin'?"

It took me a moment to translate that. His accent was a bit thick, even for one born and bred in the Cotswolds. "Er, no. No, I can hear perfectly well. You?"

"Nothin' wrong wit' my ears."

"Oh, that's a relief. I imagine your job would be quite difficult otherwise."

He gave me a look that made it clear he thought me a lunatic. "I guess. Where'd't other one get to? Can't be losin' folk in these 'ere woods."

"Oh, well, you see—"

"Just here," Chaz said, popping from around a tree. "Had to, ah... you know."

Phelps grunted in acknowledgement and strode on.

"Well?" I asked.

"He got away."

"Damnation."

"Language, love," he said, amused.

"Don't 'language' me. Now we'll never know who it was or what he wants."

"We'll just have to keep an eye out. I'm sure it was just a curious local. I doubt he meant any harm." Chaz seemed unperturbed and ready to lay the whole thing to rest.

I, on the other hand, wasn't so sure. My intuition was telling me something was amiss. And my intuition, as I'd discovered recently, was rarely wrong.

Chapter 4

I arrived back at the manor house in time to find Aunt Butty standing in the foyer, wrapping a scarf around her throat. The burnt orange cashmere matched her wide-brimmed wool hat which was festooned with an inordinate amount of burgundy and chocolate-brown ribbons.

"Where are you off to, Aunt?" I asked, padding across the cool marble in my stockinged feet. I'd left the muddy Wellies and oversized coat in the utility room and was on my way to change.

"I'm going to visit Ella Vale, my dear."

"You mean you and mummy's old nanny?" I didn't say it, but the woman must be a hundred by now. My mother had rarely talked about her former nanny, but Aunt Butty had told me copious stories.

"I do indeed. She finally retired a few years back. I bought her a cottage here, as this is where her people are from. I visit her when I can."

"I'd no idea," I murmured.

"Why would you? Anyway, I'm off. Would you like to meet her?"

"Of course. Give me five minutes." I relished the chance to meet someone who'd known Aunt Butty when she was young.

I dashed up the stairs and in no time had put my gray dress back on, wriggled into a pair of stockings, and laced up some cute little booties. My navy coat and matching cloche finished the outfit rather well, I thought.

"Going somewhere?" Binky asked as I exited my room. He was looking dusty and had a box tucked under one arm. Obviously, he'd been at Aunt Butty's beck and call whilst I was out.

"I'm off with Aunt Butty to go visit an old family retainer."

"How dull. I plan to enjoy the fire Mr. Singh has laid in the library." He hesitated. "And avoid that ghastly cousin of yours. Does she have to be here?"

"I'm not the one who invited her," I reminded him. "And you should be nice to her. She's family after all." I couldn't help taunting him just a bit. Binky had been rather vile to me over the years.

He groaned. "Maybe I can lock the library door."

"I better go. Aunt Butty is waiting."

"Hurry back," he pleaded. To which I laughed. "By the way, I couldn't help but overhear… do you think we're in danger?" He twitched a little.

"Danger?"

"From whomever is following you. You've got to admit, you do tend to get into scrapes."

"I'm sure it's nothing to worry about," I assured him, despite the fact I wasn't so sure myself. "Just a coincidence."

As I strode down the hall, I noticed one of the bedroom doors was open just a crack. As I passed, it snicked shut. I was fairly certain it was crazy cousin Olivia's room. Had she been listening in?

The thought gave me a moment's unease. What a nosy parker!

Then I brushed it off. So what if she had been? It was rude, certainly, but she could have heard nothing of importance.

I dashed down the stairs and joined Aunt Butty, determined to ignore my growing unrest.

Ella Vale lived in a tiny cottage in the heart of Sheepswick Hill. It had thick stone walls, a low thatched roof, no front garden to speak of, and a wind chime that twirled lazily in the breeze. A fat tabby sat in the window glaring at me.

Aunt Butty strode to the door and gave it a solid rap with the handle of her umbrella. The day had turned to drizzle and gloom. Typical British weather. I suddenly longed for my villa in France.

The door creaked open, and a tiny woman with snow white hair and enough wrinkles to get lost in stared up at us. She wore a long gray wool skirt, a white blouse that buttoned up to her chin, and a bright red sweater that looked handknit. Her small, blue eyes were bright and sharp, but she gave us a vague smile. "Yes?" Then she dropped the vague act. "Little Butty! Come in my dear! Who is this pretty young lady?"

"My niece. Ophelia, Lady Rample."

"Oh, dear. A widow already. And so young. Tea?" Without waiting for an answer, she turned and shuffled into the depths of the cottage.

We followed her into the kitchen where she waved us to the rough country table surrounded by mismatching chairs and covered in doilies. Apparently, our status meant nothing to her. I liked her immediately.

She bustled about the kitchen boiling water, collecting biscuits, and stacking teacups. Aunt Butty and I both offered to help, but she shooed us off with a cluck of her tongue. "I'm not dead yet."

After she'd served us all tea and we'd helped ourselves to rich tea biscuits, a particular favorite of mine with their buttery crispness, she said, "Now, tell me. Why have you come?"

"Bi-annual visit, of course," Aunt Butty said. "Plus, we're in the village for Christmas. Going to have a lovely party. Everyone's invited."

"You should come," I said.

"Oh, I don't celebrate, dear." Nanny Ella patted my hand. "Not since the Great War."

I frowned, unsure what the war had to do with anything. It had been fourteen years since it ended.

"Nanny Ella lost her only grandchild to the war," Aunt Butty said gently.

"Simon," Ella said. "Lovely boy. So young."

"Oh, I'm sorry." I meant it. I'd seen so many young men die. I still had nightmares about it sometimes, though I liked to pretend I didn't. Stiff upper lip and all that.

She patted my hand again before helping herself to another biscuit. "What's done is done. But I've no more use for Christmas."

We visited with her awhile longer, she and Aunt Butty talking of things from my aunt's childhood. Like the time she tried to put on a play for the grownups, but none of the other children would cooperate, so she played all the parts herself. Or the time she decided she could fly if she just wanted it badly enough, so she jumped out of a tree wearing a cape. Fortunately, it hadn't been a very tall tree, so she'd only broken her arm.

At last we got up to leave. It was then I noticed that above the range was a shelf holding a single photograph in a simple frame.

"Who's that?" I asked, looking closer. The face seemed familiar.

"That's my grandson, Simon," Ella said proudly. "Right before he went off to fight. Handsome, wasn't he?"

"Oh, yes," I murmured, but I barely paid attention to what she said, for I recognized Simon's face. I was almost certain he was the man who'd been following me!

Chapter 5

I arrived back at the manor in high dudgeon. The moment we'd left Ella's house I'd told my aunt that I suspected Simon was the person following me around.

"Are you certain he's the man you saw outside Harrod's?" Aunt Butty had asked, pulling on her gloves as I opened Ella's gate.

"Absolutely. It was Simon Vale. I'm sure of it now."

She'd grabbed my arm and tugged me toward the motorcar. "Well, we shan't tell Nanny. Not yet. It would break her heart if we're wrong."

I gaped at her. "But... I'm *not* wrong."

"Of course not, dear." She'd patted my hand in a condescending manner. To which I took offense. The ride home had been rather quiet.

Still feeling peeved, I'd had dinner in my room. I'd even eschewed cocktail hour—almost unheard of for me—although Chaz did come up after dinner, an Irish coffee in hand. Minus the coffee.

"Here you are, old thing," he said, handing me the drink before taking a seat at my dressing table and idly sifting through my lipsticks. The cases made little clacking sounds.

"Can you believe she thinks I'm making things up?" I asked after taking a deep swallow. The liquor burned itself all the way to my belly.

"I doubt she thinks that," he soothed.

I snorted. "She thinks I've lost my mind and am hallucinating or something. She quite literally told me I've an overactive imagination."

"Which is why I'm amused."

I gave him a narrow look. "What are you saying?"

"Ophelia, you and your aunt are two peas of a pod. Which is way I find it all highly entertaining."

Unfortunately, I didn't have a comeback for that. "Well, it was uncalled for," I said rather lamely.

"Of course, dearest," he soothed. But his upper lip was still twitching.

"Anyway, did she tell you that our creeper is none other than Ella Vale's grandson who died during the war?"

"She did. He's obviously not dead."

"Obviously," I said drily, draining my glass.

"If he truly is Simon," he pointed out infuriatingly.

"He is," I insisted. I was utterly certain of it by this point.

"All right let's say he is. Why do you suppose he hasn't gone home to his grandmother? Let her know he's alive? It's the first thing I would do. Where has he been all this time since the war ended?"

"God knows," I said. "A lot of men were so traumatized by what happened over there that they just can't function normally anymore. Which is why I'm leery of the fact he keeps popping up. He could be unstable."

"All the more reason to help him, don't you think?"

"I do. Unless, of course, he means me harm." I frowned. "And I can't imagine why he'd be sneaking around otherwise."

"People do all sorts of strange things for all sorts of strange reasons," he pointed out.

"You aren't wrong there. Well, I'm to bed. Get along with you."

"This early? Surely not."

"Don't be facetious. I've had a long and trying day."

He snickered on his way out.

It took me a long time to fall asleep. When I did, it was restless and full of dreams. Not particularly pleasant ones.

I dreamt I was back in the ward during the war. I'd been a training nurse assigned to one of the make-shift hospitals that had sprung up all over the country in an attempt to treat the wounded soldiers pouring in from the battle field. So many of them hadn't made it.

I walked the ward, offering cups of water to the dying. The occasional prayer to a god I didn't much believe in anymore. Soothing a fevered brow.

At the end of the row lay a young soldier. He couldn't have been more than eighteen. Half his face was wrapped in bandages. He moaned in pain.

"You gotta help him."

I turned to the soldier in the next bed and my eyes widened. It was Simon Vale, the boy in Ella's photograph. The man who'd been following me. Had I inserted him into my dream? Or had he really been there?

"I'm sorry." My heart broke. "There's nothing I can do." He's dying. But I didn't say it aloud.

Simon grabbed my arm, fingers digging into my flesh. "Save him, or you will regret it."

I jarred awake to moonlight streaming into my room. Sweat soaked and heart racing, I sat up and switched on the light.

I remembered now.

The boy who'd died.

The friend who'd begged me to save him.

I hadn't dreamt him. He'd been there. In that ward. And when his friend had died...

Simon Vale had threatened my life.

The next morning, I overslept. Without Maddie to bring me tea, throw open the curtains, and demand I get up immediately, I had a tendency to sleep rather late. The fire had been made up while I slept, and the room was surprisingly cozy.

I managed to hoist myself to a sitting position, legs dangling off the side of the bed. I slid my feet into my slippers, then let out a shriek.

My door banged open and Chaz, looking mussed and half asleep, barged in, Binky behind him. There was a chorus of "What happened?" and "What's going on?"

I pointed at my slipper. "There's something in there."

Chaz snatched the slipper from the floor and held it upside down. Something small, furry, and still fell out and hit the floor with a plop.

"Good heavens, it's a dead rat!" Aunt Butty peered around Binky, still in her dressing gown, hair wrapped up in a sleeping cap and cold cream smeared across her face.

"Not a rat," Chaz assured her. "Just a mouse. But it is definitely dead."

"Probably crawled in there and died," Binky said. "I'll have the servants dispose of it."

Chaz gave him a disgusted look. "I can manage." He scooped the thing up by its tail and marched from the room.

"Be sure and wash your hands thoroughly," Aunt Butty called after him. "You never know where that disgusting thing has been."

"If that's all, I'm off for my morning constitutional," Binky said, glancing down the hall behind him. More likely he was trying to escape Olivia who'd yet to put in an appearance.

I noticed he was dressed for walking. "Your concern is noted." I said dryly.

"It was a dead mouse, Ophelia. Nothing to get excited about." He rolled his eyes in a Binky-like fashion that made him look increasingly beaver-like.

"You'll have to throw away those slippers. It's unsanitary," Aunt Butty said as Binky strode from the room. "I'll have Flora burn them, if she can manage it without setting the house on fire. You can borrow a pair of mine. I brought extra."

"Thank you, Aunt Butty," I said with a shudder of revulsion. "I don't think that mouse crawled in there and died of its own accord."

She sat beside me on the bed. "What do you mean?"

"I think it was Simon."

"Why would Simon Vale—if it is him you've been seeing—put a dead mouse in your slipper? And how in blazes would he get in the house?"

I told her about my dream and how I remembered meeting Simon during the war. "He was very angry when his friend died. It couldn't be helped. No one's fault but the Germans. His wounds were simply too extensive. All we could do was keep him as comfortable as possible and..."

"And wait," Aunt Butty said softly. "Sometimes that's all there is." She squeezed my hand.

"I didn't blame him. Simon, I mean. For being angry. I can't image how hard it must have been for him. Watching a mate die like that. Nothing he could do. All that pain and anger had to go somewhere."

"Better putting it on the Germans," Aunt Butty said stoutly.

I shrugged. "I know. But that's how it is sometimes I suppose."

"But this was years ago, Ophelia. Let us assume it was him. Why would he follow you from London, sneak in the house, and put a dead mouse in your slipper?"

"It sounds a little ridiculous when you put it like that," I admitted. A little niggle of unease settled in. There was, after all, another person who could be guilty. But no. It must be an outsider. "But who else would do it? No, I think he's trying to get revenge."

"That's your guilt talking." Aunt Butty gave me a knowing look.

My hackles went up a bit. "What do I have to be guilty for?"

"Nothing. But that isn't how guilt works, is it? You can't save everyone, Ophelia."

Perhaps not. But I could try.

Chapter 6

Later that day, I decided it was time to make a concerted effort to find Simon. I knew without a doubt he was around somewhere. Plus, it gave me an excuse to skip out on decorating while avoiding my ghastly cousin.

Olivia had spent the morning alternatively fawning over Binky and Chaz. Chaz, knowing exactly what sort of game she was playing and possibly because it amused him, played right into it, flirting back like mad. She kept shooting me victorious looks as if she'd stolen my love away from me. Which was comical.

Binky, on the other hand, was terrified of her. He tried to escape every chance he got. He even walked out on her in the middle of a sentence and was generally blatantly rude. I'd feel sorry for him if he wasn't such a twit. Her annoyance amused me even more.

"Poor Olivia. She is in a house with possibly the only two men in England she can't wrap around her little finger," Aunt Butty had observed. "Well, she might be able to wrap Binky if he wasn't so terrified of her."

"Why did you invite her?" I asked. "She's not terribly nice."

"To be honest, she invited herself," Aunt Butty admitted. "I got a letter from her a couple weeks ago and, well, the more the merrier, am I right?"

"In this instance, I don't think so," I said dryly.

She laughed. "True. But it's only over Christmas, then she's back to whence she came."

"Aces," I muttered before excusing myself. The game, as they say, was afoot.

My first stop was the kitchen. The servants always seem to know everything that goes on. Flora was there, digging into a hunk of cake, while the cook was bustling about the kitchen. I probably should chastise Flora for not being about her duties, but it wasn't my place. If Aunt Butty didn't mind her maid eating cake when she should be ironing, who was I to say differently?

"Cook, Flora, I was wondering if either of you have seen a strange man lurking about."

Flora stared at me, mouth half full of cake. "Cor, blimey, miss. Is it another one of them murderers you're always finding? We're going to be killed in our beds!" The last ended on a wail so loud, that Cook was forced to clap her hands over her ears.

When the wailing didn't stop immediately, Cook smacked her along the backside of the head. Flora shut up and shoved another bite of cake in her mouth.

"No, my lady, we 'aven't. Not 'round here. Now if you don't mind, got things to do." And Cook presented her broad back to me. Apparently, the discussion was over.

I called my thanks and exited quickly, not willing to risk her wrath. I didn't want cut off from her excellent cakes.

The char woman who came in every day from the village was polishing the floor of the entry hall. She claimed ignorance as well. Which left only the outside staff.

I dashed upstairs and exchanged my pumps for fur-lined boots and threw on a thick, wool wrap, also edged in fur. I didn't bother with hat or gloves. I wasn't going far, and I wouldn't be long. From my bedroom window, I could see the gardener and his helper tending to the walled garden.

I hurried outside and down the path to where the red brick wall loomed. Halfway down, a green painted door stood open.

Surprisingly, it was several degrees warmer inside the garden, and I loosened my wrap a bit. Despite the lateness of the year, there were still green plants hugging the wall, perfuming the air with the scent of herbs.

When I repeated my questions, the head gardener tugged on his cap. "Wull, I found some footprints inna beds this morning."

I struggled to translate that. Flower beds. Must be. "Which ones?"

"Up'ta house."

"What size?"

He scratched the side of his nose. "Eh?"

"What size were the prints? Large like a man's?"

"Oh, aye."

"But you didn't see anyone?"

He mulled it over. "Nope."

I glanced at the gardener's helper, but he, too, shook his head. This was going exactly nowhere. "Thank you. Do you know where the groundskeeper, Mr. Phelps, is?"

The gardener pointed randomly in the direction of the woods. I might have known. I did not fancy going into the woods alone but needs must.

Bracing myself, I strode on, channeling my inner Aunt Butty. Aunt Butty was a force to be reckoned with. She'd once faced down the Kaiser, before he was the Kaiser, but still. Apparently, while visiting Germany at the tender age of eighteen, young Aunt Butty had crashed a party thrown in Wilhelm's honor. When he discovered she hadn't been invited and tried to have her thrown out, she'd challenged him to a drinking contest. Which she'd won. The woman would not be cowed by a spooky forest.

What I wouldn't give for one of Aunt Butty's cocktails right about now.

Shadows loomed long, like crone's fingers reaching out to grab me. The wind made an odd whistling noise like the distant lonesome call of a steam engine. I clutched my fur collar more tightly about my throat and wished I'd brought gloves and a hat after all.

Something flitted at the edge of my vision. I quickly turned my head, but there was nothing there. I shivered as if a ghost had passed over my grave, then I cursed my overactive imagination.

Unless I wasn't imagining. "Simon Vale, I know you're there." My voice came out less... impressive than I could have wished. I cleared my throat and tried again. "Simon, come out here at once. Show yourself!"

Was that a giggle? I craned to see, but the thicket was too dense.

"Watchur yellin' for, milady?"

I nearly jumped out of my skin as Mr. Phelps appeared out of nowhere, face ruddy with cold.

"Oh, there you are. I was looking for you."

He tugged on his cap. "Well, you found me."

I quickly told him my suspicions about Simon Vale lurking about the grounds. "He could be dangerous, you know."

"Simon?" The groundskeeper snorted. "Knew that boy when 'e was a lad. Ain't got a harmful bone in 'is body."

I stiffened my spine. "And yet he left a dead rodent in my slipper this morning."

He arched a brow. "That I doubt."

"You think I'm lying?"

"No, milady. But it weren't Simon wot done it. You can be sure o' that."

"Be that as it may, have you seen him?"

He tugged on his cap again. "No, milady, can't say as I 'ave. But I'll keep an eye out."

"Thank you," I said, albeit a little stiffly.

I stomped back to the house, my mind a whirl. Despite Mr. Phelps's assurances, I was certain it was Simon who'd left the rodent. It had to be. I didn't like to think of another option.

"Somebody get me a whiskey!" I sank onto the chaise longue in the parlor with every ounce of drama I could muster.

"How about some wassail? I had Cook whip some up. It's delicious. She put extra cinnamon in it." Without waiting for a response, Aunt Butty poured a large serving of the fragrant beverage and handed it to me.

"It's a bit early for wassailing, isn't it?" I asked, accepting the cup.

She snorted. "I don't hold with all that truck, but I do love some spiced wine."

Any excuse, I supposed. I took a sip and nearly choked. While deliciously sweet and spicy, the drink was strong enough to put hair on an ox.

"What exactly is in your wassail recipe, Aunt?"

"Hmmm?" she murmured distractedly as she carefully strung holly along the mantle, eyeing her handiwork critically. "The usual. Cloves, sugar, apples, oranges. Possibly nutmeg. I left it up to Cook."

"No, I mean the booze."

"Oh, that. Cider, of course. Local stuff. Excellent kick. Port, sherry, bit of rum."

"More than a bit, I'd say." I downed another swallow. It wasn't whiskey, but it was growing on me.

"How did your search go?" She rummaged around in a crate of Christmas decorations which was perched on a side table, occasionally pulling out random bits and pieces.

"Precisely nowhere," I admitted. "No one has seen Simon anywhere."

She slid me a look. "Perhaps you're barking up the wrong tree. Here. Help me."

I stood up as she thrust pieces of a miniature nativity scene at me. "I thought you didn't hold with this stuff." I waved a plaster of Paris camel at her. It had been neatly hand-painted brown with a garish yellow and green saddle.

"I don't. Stuff and nonsense. But this is an old-fashioned village with old-fashioned people. Must make them feel comfortable."

It was the first time I'd ever heard my aunt even consider other people's feelings on the matter of religion. Perhaps she was mellowing.

"Let's go set this up in the hall." She marched out of the room, clutching a handful of colorful figurines to her ample bosom.

We'd just finished our mission and had refreshed our wassail when Chaz returned with my ghastly cousin. He held a surprisingly large ball of mistletoe in one hand and was trying to fend off Olivia's advances with his other.

She, meanwhile, was cooing and batting her lashes at him like a ninny. If only the idiot knew the truth, but it wasn't my truth to tell, so I remained silent, chortling to myself.

"I'm going to change into something more comfortable. Be sure and hang that mistletoe in a convenient location, Chaz, darling!" She giggled and did a little finger wave before sashaying upstairs. If one with no hips could sashay.

"Can't you get rid of her, Aunt Butty?" I asked.

"That would be rude." Aunt Butty frowned at a tangle of tinsel she was attempting to unravel. "I don't know what happened to her. She was such a nice, quiet child."

"She's certainly neither of those things now," Chaz said dryly. "Where do you want this?" He jiggled the ball of mistletoe up and down.

"Stick it on the hall table for now," Aunt Butty said. "I'll have Mr. Singh hang it later. And help yourself to wassail. I think Cook finally got the recipe just right."

After divesting himself of the mistletoe, he helped himself to a large cup of wassail. One sip and he grimaced. "It's a bit... strong."

"No sense making wassail if it doesn't get one three sheets to the wind before suppertime," Aunt Butty assured him as she hauled out boxes of glass balls from the crates. "Help me with this tree."

Chaz took another sip before he obligingly helped hang the Christmas decorations. "Might have too much cinnamon."

"You think?" Aunt Butty frowned in thought. "I think it makes it... Christmassy."

"Perhaps you should try eggnog next," he suggested, hanging a light blue ball dusted in gold next to a silver star.

Her eyes brightened. "Oh, rum. I do love rum!"

While they continued their discussion of rum whilst trimming the tree, I slipped into the hall to make a phone call.

There was one person who might answer my questions about Simon Vale.

Lord Peter Varant was a member of my social circle, did something mysterious for the government, was a sometime assistant in my investigations, and had often expressed some interest in my person. Although we had been to dinner once or twice, our calendars rarely seemed to match up and nothing much ever came of it. And then there was Hale, of course. Who, up until recently, had been of far more interest to me.

Varant picked up the telephone himself. "Ophelia, to what do I owe this pleasure?"

"You're answering your own phone these days? Shocking."

"I gave the butler some time off," he said dryly. "Couldn't have him moping about here over the holidays."

"Of course not. And you?"

"I was going to go up to my sister's, but... you know how it goes."

I didn't, actually, but I assumed it had something to do with his secret work for the government. "Listen, can you find out some information for me on a soldier?"

There was a pause. "The military likes to keep that sort of thing close to the vest."

"I don't think he's in anymore. He served during the Great War."

"Ah, yes. Well, perhaps. Details?" A chair on the other end of the line as if he'd taken a seat.

"Simon Vale. Current age, perhaps mid-thirties. From the village of Sheepswick Hill in the Cotswolds."

I could hear the scratch of his pencil as he took notes. "I'll do what I can. How urgent is this?"

"Fairly urgent, but not life threatening. Probably."

"That sounds grim. Happy Christmas, Ophelia." And he'd rung off before I could tell him the same.

As I made my way back to the drawing room, I caught movement on the stairs. I looked up to see a bit of red fabric disappearing around the corner. Olivia. It had to be. She must have been listening in on my call. But why?

I doubted it was important. Anything I told Varant would mean nothing to her. I gave a mental shrug and rejoined the tree trimming party.

Chapter 7

Christmas Eve, the day of the party, dawned bright and clear. Aunt Butty bemoaned the fact that there was no snow as she supervised Cook's latest attempt at wassail.

"It's hardly Christmas without snow."

"It's not like this is the first Christmas it hasn't snowed," I reminded her, peering into the pot. It smelled heavenly. Sweet, citrusy, and spicy. My mouth watered in anticipation.

"I know, but it doesn't feel nearly as festive. More orange."

Cook shot her a look but dropped in a few more wedges and gave the pot a vigorous stir. "Shouldn't you be wrapping gifts or somethin,' Milady."

"Oh, dear, yes. I'd forgotten. Don't forget to add the port." And she scurried off while I filched a mini mince pie from the cooling rack before scampering off myself.

In the hall, I saw Olivia supervising Binky's hanging of the mistletoe. I was surprised Mr. Singh hadn't hung it. But perhaps he'd been busy with other endeavors. As I passed the two, Olivia gave me a smug look. I tried very hard not to roll my eyes.

Half the guests had already arrived when I made my way downstairs that evening to join the party. It'd taken longer than usual to get ready without Maddie's help.

I'd chosen a cream gown which gathered at the waist and crisscrossed over the bodice. The draping effect gave the impression of a Grecian costume. I wore my ruby jewelry to offset it. They'd been a gift from Felix our first Christmas together. I'd had to go with a fairly simple wave as I could only do so much to my hair without it turning into a disaster, but it was neatly held with a ruby pin I'd found at Harrods that went well with the set.

Olivia was already in the drawing room and stared daggers at me. She herself was dressed in a rather cheap and gawdy red gown with white trim. I tried not to be too judgmental. After all, she wasn't exactly loaded, for all her airs and graces.

Most of the other guests were villagers dressed in their Sunday best. The local vicar brayed loudly over some joke, his cheeks already flushed with drink.

Aunt Butty and Chaz had finished the Christmas tree and it glittered festively while a yule log burned in the grate. A small local quartet played lively music in the corner and partygoers milled out drinking Seventh Heaven cocktails, the pink liquid sweet and refreshing. They nibbled on mini minced pies, spicy Christmas cookies, and bite-sized Christmas cake while gossiping about the latest village scandal. Just then, Cook, dressed in her best uniform with a starched white apron, wheeled out a tray with the wassail bowl. A cheer went up as Mr. Singh and cook began serving the wassail. Aunt Butty tinked on her glass with the edge of a spoon.

"Welcome, everyone, to Sheepswick Hall! I want to wish all of you a very Happy Christmas."

Everyone cheered and lifted their glasses of wassail in a toast.

I went to take a sip, but it smelled... off. So I took the tiniest bit. Yes, something was very wrong.

"Stop!" I shouted above the music. I kicked off my shoes and clambered up on top of the coffee table with all the elegance of a mountain goat. "Stop! Don't drink!"

The music tapered off on a discordant note.

"Ophelia, what is the meaning of this?" Aunt Butty demanded.

"Don't anyone drink the wassail."

"Whyever not?" Chaz asked.

"It's been poisoned."

Chapter 8

Everyone stared at me.

Olivia, damn her eyes, let out a titter. "Don't be daft, Ophelia. You do love being the center of attention, don't you?" Her eyes were small and beady, glittering with maliciousness. My distrust of her grew tenfold.

"I'm telling you, there is something not right with this punch."

Aunt Butty took a sip and made a face. "She's right. This isn't my recipe. Mr. Singh! Collect all the wassail. Make sure no one drinks it. I'm getting to the bottom of this."

She marched down the hall with Chaz, Binky, and me on her heels. Olivia trotted along behind us.

"This is nonsense," Olivia muttered. "Ophelia is having hysterics."

Aunt Butty whirled on her. "Maybe she is and maybe she isn't, but until we discover the truth, you will kindly shut your mouth."

Olivia looked like she'd sucked on a lemon. But she shut her mouth.

In the kitchen, Cook and Flora were busy filling trays with more mini mince pies. Cook glanced up and her face grew red. "Wot's this then?" Intruding on her domain was not something Aunt Butty usually did. Well, except for when making wassail.

"There is something wrong with the wassail," Aunt Butty announced, marching to the cooker.

"No there ain't." Cook's face flushed red in outrage. "I made it exactly like you said. Look for yourself. Big pot."

Aunt Butty lifted the lid of the largest pot. "What are these little white things? Those aren't in my recipe."

Both Cook and I rushed over, vying for a peek. I won through sheer determination.

"They look like mistletoe berries," I pointed out.

Cook practically shoved her face into the pot. "I didn't put them in. Did you?" She whirled to glare accusingly at Flora who blanched.

"No, Cook. Even I know them'll make people sick."

76

"Worse," Cook grumbled. "It could kill folks. Though there don't look enough here for that, less'n someone has a weak constitution."

"Probably just a prank," Olivia offered. I noticed she was the only one who didn't rush to poke her nose in the wassail pot. Even Chaz and Binky were straining to see over Cook's ample form.

"Some prank." I glared at Olivia. "People could have *died*. That's attempted murder."

"Maybe it was that Simon person you've been looking for," Olivia offered.

"Sure," Chaz snorted. "A total stranger snuck into the kitchen and dumped poisonous berries in the stew? Not likely."

"How do you know about Simon?" I demanded.

"Oh, one hears things," she said airily. "Well, I'm back to the party." And she strutted out like she was some sort of film star. Looking confused, Binky wandered after her.

Chaz leaned in close. "I don't trust that one."

"Nor do I. She's up to something."

"Come, you two," Aunt Butty ordered. "We must calm our guests. Cook, make sure every drop of that wassail is destroyed, then get started on a new batch. In the meantime, I'll send Mr. Singh for the eggnog."

Cook rolled her eyes. "Yes, Milady."

The guests were surprisingly calm about the whole thing. The band was playing something upbeat and festive. Several couples danced. Mr. Singh brought out the eggnog—fortunately untainted—to appease the masses. All was going swimmingly.

Still, I kept an eye on Olivia. What was she up to? And how did she know about Simon?

I remembered the flash of red on the stairs after I'd called Varant. It was clear she'd been eavesdropping. The sly little minx. Still, she could have heard nothing of import because there was nothing of import to know. Not yet, at least.

Was she right? Was Simon still so angry over the death of his friend that he'd tried not only to poison me, but an entire houseful of guests? Was he really that unhinged?

The man I'd seen on the street and later in the village hadn't appeared that way. Sad, yes. Forlorn, definitely. But he had looked neither angry nor insane. And it seemed to me that whoever spiked the punch had to be one or both.

It was the wee morning hours, and several rounds of Christmas carols, before the final guests climbed into their motorcars and trundled off into the dark. I was somewhat relieved. It had been hard to enjoy oneself when thoughts of attempted murder loomed.

I said goodnight to Chaz, Binky, and Aunt Butty—Olivia had gone up a couple hours earlier claiming headache. More likely, she was tired of being ignored by our very married neighbors. There hadn't been a single eligible man among them. As I climbed the stairs, exhaustion weighed me down. I was bone tired, but sleep felt far away. How could I possibly rest when there was a madman on the loose?

I pushed open my bedroom door, flipped on the light, and stared, mouth hanging open. "Oh, dear."

Backing out of the room, I slowly made my way down the stairs. Aunt Butty and Chaz glanced up as I entered the room. Binky was snoring softly on the sofa and didn't stir.

"What is it, Ophelia? You're white as a sheet," Aunt Butty asked.

"I, ah, think you'd better come upstairs," I said. "There's something in my room you should see."

"Not another dead mouse," Chaz groaned.

"Worse."

Aunt Butty went a little pale, but in true Aunt Butty fashion, she marched through the doorway, up the stairs, and into my room. "Good heavens!"

Chaz stopped in the doorway. "Well, that's not on, is it?"

"What's going on?" Olivia's voice came from behind me. "What's all the noise about? You woke me up." She didn't look like she'd just woken up. She looked like she'd just finished touching up her makeup.

"Have a look." I motioned her into the room.

There, painted in red dripping letters on the wall above my bed was the word, DIE. Nothing more, nothing less.

Aunt Butty frowned. "Is that—"

"Blood," I said. "A warning. Written in blood."

Chapter 9

"It's not blood," Mr. Singh assured me with his usual unshakeable calm. "It's ink."

"You're sure? It looks like blood."

"I believe it has been mixed with something to make it thicker, but the scent is unmistakable."

I leaned over the bed and gave the wall a whiff. Sure enough, the unmistakable sharp tang of ink hit my nose. I breathed a sigh of relief. Ink was definitely better than blood.

"Can you get it off the wallpaper?" Aunt Olivia asked. "I don't want to have to pay to redecorate this room."

Mr. Singh bowed. "I will do my best, my lady."

"You'll have to sleep in one of the other guest rooms, Ophelia. I'll have Flora make one up for you."

"Thank you, but I don't think I can sleep now. I'll wait until Mr. Singh is finished. For now, I'll go help myself to some hot milk." And whiskey. Loads of whiskey.

As I passed Olivia, she smirked as if she enjoyed my discomfort. Frankly, I couldn't wait to be rid of her.

Christmas Day dawned bright and clear. Still no snow, despite the nip in the air.

I was just passing through the hall when the telephone rang. I glanced around, expecting Mr. Singh to put in an appearance, but he did not. Most unusual. So I picked up the 'phone myself.

"Sheepswick Hall."

"Ophelia. It's Varant." His voice oozed warmth through the line. "Happy Christmas."

"Varant! Happy Christmas. What have you found out?"

"I was unable to find anything about Simon Vale's current whereabouts."

Of course not. Because he was following me around. "Go on."

"But I did discover something about his war record." There was a shuffle of papers. "After he was released from the hospital where you met him, he was shipped back to the front."

"Dear heavens, poor man." To lose his friend and then be sent back… I shuddered at the thought.

"After returning to the front, he comported himself with great honor, even saving several of his platoon during a firefight with the Germans."

That was a surprise. "He's a war hero."

"Indeed."

"Anything else?"

"Nothing except a letter informing his grandmother of his death."

"He's not dead."

He didn't ask if I was certain. "Then that needs to be rectified."

After thanking Varant, I hung up and stood for a moment, taking it in. Everything I thought about Simon had been wrong. So what did that mean?

I shook my head slightly. I needed coffee and a moment to think things through.

As I made my way to the breakfast room, the scents of cinnamon and vanilla and frying bacon wafted from the kitchen.

I helped myself to fresh coffee and a sticky bun, ignored the large plate of smoked salmon, and took more than my fair share of bacon. As I settled in to enjoy my food, Olivia strode into the room. My mood immediately took a downturn.

"Oh, you're up." Her expression was constipated. No other word for it. "I was hoping Chaz would agree to a Christmas morning ramble. So good for the constitution." She poured herself a cup of tea.

"If you say so." I was not fond of rambles or any other form of exertion. "I'm afraid Chaz is still abed."

"Not so, old thing." Chaz appeared, looking fresh as the proverbial daisy. He leaned down to give me a peck on the cheek. "I could smell Cook's sticky buns for miles. And you're looking none the worse for wear after your trying evening. Mr. Singh was able to remove the ink, I take it?"

"Near enough. Aunt Butty is having him move a picture today so as to hide the pink stain it left behind."

"Dreadful business," he said. "Wonder what that chap was thinking."

"These commoners are nothing but a nuisance." Olivia sat across from me with nothing but her tea which she sipped delicately while shooting Chaz coy glances.

I didn't bother to bring up Simon's status as war hero. I doubted it would impress her.

"We're not eating?" I asked tartly.

"Some of us like to keep trim figures," she said, eyeing my more generous curves with derision.

Naturally I was forced to take an enormous bite of sticky bun. I wasn't forced to moan in pleasure, but I did anyway, just to see her features twist. "Too bad. More for me."

Her fingers gripped her cup a little too hard, and for the first time I noticed her hands were a bit pinker than they should be. I frowned and opened my mouth to say something, but before I could, Mr. Singh arrived. And he wasn't alone.

For struggling in his grip, and cursing up a storm, was none other than Simon Vale.

Chapter 10

We all stared at Simon. He was grubby with dark circles under his eyes and he smelled strongly of hay.

"He's been hiding in the stables, my lady," Mr. Singh said.

"All the better to torture you, dear Ophelia," Olivia said, though her tone was distinctly lacking in sympathy to the point of sounding amused. I shot her a glare.

"What is going on?" Aunt Butty cried, arriving in a morning gown she'd had specially made for Christmas. It was Kelly green with little red and white spots all over it and trimmed out in red. It was, surprisingly, on the tame side for her. What wasn't tame was the enormous felt hair piece made to look like holly leaves and berries.

"Mr. Singh has captured our harasser," Chaz said calmly, digging into a plate of smoked salmon and toast.

"I'm not a harasser," Simon howled.

"You put a dead rat in Ophelia's shoe!" Aunt Butty accused.

"Did not."

"It was a mouse, Aunt Butty. In my slipper," I corrected.

"Mouse. Rat. I didn't do it!" Simon said.

"Then there was that ghastly message on your wall," Olivia said calmly, her pink fingers strumming on the side of her cup.

"I haven't even been in the house. How could I write a message on your wall?" Simon shouted.

"Enough!" I sliced the air with my hand. "Mr. Singh. Could you please escort Mr. Vale to the kitchen and get him something to eat? He looks half starved. I will deal with him later." Because war hero or not, I still had questions.

"You're going to feed your harasser?" Olivia said. "Not very bright, cousin. This is how people that that get above their station."

Oh, that Olivia was a nasty piece of work.

I gave Mr. Singh a meaningful look. He nodded and escorted a protesting Simon out.

"It's Christmas, Olivia. A time for kindness, don't you think?" I arched a brow as I gazed at her over a bite of sticky bun.

"If you say so." Her tone told me she thought I was being an idiot.

"Your fingers are pink, Olivia."

Her fingers stilled their restless strumming as she stared down at them and then back at me. "So?"

"It happens to be the precise shade of pink that my walls were once Mr. Singh removed the ink. Or rather, attempted to remove the ink. He's a whiz at most things, but that ink was particularly stubborn."

Aunt Butty and Chaz watched our back and forth like a game of tennis.

"So?" Olivia laughed. "I had an accident with a bottle of nail varnish. It's nothing to do with you or that stupid message."

"Isn't it? After all, these things only started happening after you arrived," I pointed out.

She laughed again, a slight edge of hysteria to her tone. "You said it yourself. You had a harasser. He's the one who did those things. He was here."

"I don't think so," I said calmly. "Yes, he was here. But he arrived the same day I did. I saw him in the village. And nothing happened. Not until *you* arrived. That's when the dead mouse appeared. That's when the message was written in ink on my wall. Even now, Mr. Singh is going through your things. What do you think he'll find?"

"You have no right!" she screeched.

"But I do," Aunt Butty said. "My name is on the lease. Therefore, this is my house, albeit temporarily."

"Well, he will find nothing. Do you hear me? Nothing. You can't prove anything." This time her laugh was brittle as she shoved her chair from the table and rose, throwing her napkin down next to her cup which rattled in protest. Her eyes narrowed to little slits. "Whatever happened to you, you had coming."

"Whatever did I do to you?" I asked.

"You got to live the life I should have had," she hissed. "Why should *you* have all the money? All these men fawning over you? Everyone thinks you're so marvelous. Well, you're not. And everyone's going to know about it."

"I think you should leave now, Olivia," Aunt Butty said calmly but firmly. "You're no longer welcome in this house, or any other."

"Fine! I don't want to be here anyway." And with that, she marched off. We could hear her slamming around upstairs.

"If she did all those things, you should have her arrested," Chaz said around a mouthful of smoked salmon. He hadn't stopped eating through the whole thing.

"We cannot, I'm afraid." Mr. Singh had reentered the room so silently it made me jump. He handed me a bottle. It was empty save for a bit of dried red ink. "I found this in the refuse bin out back. It's been wiped clean of prints."

I'd no idea how Mr. Singh knew how to dust for prints, but that was a question for another day.

"No sign of any dead rodents, I suppose?" Chaz drawled.

"Nothing. There is rat poison in the kitchen, but anyone could have snuck in and got some during the night, killed a rodent, and placed it where you would find it," Mr. Singh said.

I sighed. "So no proof of her perfidy."

"I am certain you are correct and she's the one behind it all, but no. No proof that would stand up in court," he admitted.

"I wonder what her issue with you is," Chaz mused. "Surely she can't just hate you because you're..." he waved a fork. "You."

Aunt Butty sighed. "Rumor is her mother was a little... off. Not our side, of course. But perhaps Olivia inherited it." She turned to me. "I'm sorry, Ophelia, but I'd hoped that the two of you would have a lot in common. Alas, I was wrong."

"It's alright, Aunt. Happens to the best of us sometimes."

"What should I do with Mr. Vale?" Mr. Singh asked.

"Once he's had a chance to eat and clean up, bring him to the drawing room," I said. "I still want to know why he was following me."

"Very good, my lady." He bowed and strode from the room.

Binky took that very moment to appear, rubbing his eyes and yawning. "Happy Christmas, all. What'd I miss?"

I sniffed the cup of wassail suspiciously before taking a sip. It smelled fine. Tasted fine.

"I already checked it for mistletoe berries and that ghastly cousin of yours left an hour ago," Chaz assured me as he joined me on the sofa with his own cup.

"Before we open gifts, I think we should talk to Simon, don't you?" Aunt Butty sat in an armchair next to the fire. "I, for one, would feel much better about celebrating once we get this all cleared up."

I nodded. "Agreed."

Mr. Singh was sent to fetch Simon from the kitchen where, apparently, Cook was foisting half our Christmas dinner on him. I stared at the prettily decorated tree and sipped at my beverage, my mind elsewhere. I wondered what Hale was doing right now. Then I told myself I was an idiot. *Enjoy the moment.*

Mr. Singh arrived with Simon in tow. He was almost unrecognizable from the rather drooping figure we'd seen earlier. He was clean, shaved, hair trimmed, and dressed in decent clothes which I could only assume had been liberated from a wardrobe somewhere in the manor.

"Simon Vale?" I asked, setting down my cup.

He nodded. "Yes, ma'am. How'd you know?"

"It's *my lady*," Aunt Butty interrupted. "And I know your grandmother."

"How is she? Is she alright?"

Aunt Butty waved him silent. "She's fine. Which you would know if you bothered visiting her." Her expression was fierce and judgmental.

Simon had the grace to blush. "I would've, but I'd something to do first."

"Like follow me around?" I demanded. "Why?"

"Don't you remember?" He stared at me intently. "That Christmas in 1914? The same Christmas as the cease fire?"

The night of the Christmas truce when German, French, and British soldiers had laid down their weapons, crossed the trenches, and celebrated together. *Silent night, holy night…*

"Yes. I do remember. And I'm sorry your friend died, but it wasn't my fault. Harassing me won't bring him back!"

His mouth rounded in an oh shape. "Oh, my lady, I wasn't harassing you. I mean, I don't blame you for Billy's death."

I crossed my arms. "You sure did back then."

He shuffled his feet. "Back then I was young and stupid and angry. I blamed a lot of people for a lot of things. But I realize now, you did all you could. So, I came here to tell you thank you. And I'm sorry."

I blinked. "Maybe you better start at the beginning."

He nodded. "Well, you know what happened that night."

"Billy died of his wounds," I said softly. "There was nothing anyone could do, but you were very... distraught."

He smiled ruefully. "That's a kind way to put it, my lady. I was angry. I blamed you. I remember yelling a lot. Saying some pretty terrible things."

"That's in the past," I assured him. I certainly never thought about it. Well, rarely.

"Still, it was wrong, and I'm sorry."

"Apology accepted," I said. "What happened after that?"

He shrugged. "I got better. They sent me back to the front. Eventually, the war ended, and I was shipped back home."

"You were a war hero," I said. Then explained for the others. "Varant told me he saved several men from his platoon."

Simon shrugged. "I just did what any man would do. Only... only, I was such a mess after it all, you know? I couldn't face Gran like that. And I was still angry. I drank a lot. Fought a lot. Got locked up a time or two."

"Sounds rough," Chaz said softly.

"You fought?" Simon asked.

Chaz was silent a moment. "In my way."

I slid him a look. He'd never talked before about what he'd done during the war. Apparently, he wasn't going to now.

I cleared my throat. "So you stayed in London?"

Simon nodded. "I finally got my act together. Got a job. Then the depression hit, and I was out of a job. Living rough. Then one day I saw you and I remembered."

I winced. "How angry you were."

"No." He shook his head. "How sorry I was for being a bast—for being less than a gentleman back then. My Gran would be ashamed of me. She raised me better."

"Why didn't you go home to your Gran?" Aunt Butty demanded. "Why did you follow Lady Rample?"

"Because I couldn't go home to my Gran the way I was... filthy. Jobless. I thought... I thought maybe if I came to you. Explained things. Maybe you could help me find a job. Then I could go home to Gran and she'd be proud of me."

I blinked. "Your gran thinks you're dead."

He blanched. "What?"

"You never came home and then she got some letter from the Home Office. It was a mistake, of course, but she thinks you're dead."

He looked a bit wobbly. Fortunately, Mr. Singh shoved a straight-backed chair under him before he fell over.

"I never thought... I never..." He ran his hands through his hair until it stood up wildly. "Look, I'm sorry. About everything. But I swear I never did anything to hurt you. I never would have done. I need to go to my Gran right this minute."

"I agree," Aunt Butty said, setting down her cup and heaving herself to her feet. "But first, Mr. Singh, have Cook pack a hamper of Christmas goodies for Simon to take with him."

"Yes, my lady." Mr. Singh turned and strode out of the room, intent on his mission.

Simon stared at Aunt Butty with wide eyes. "But... but... it's not Boxing Day." The day after Christmas when the rich packed up their leftovers and gave them to the poor.

She laughed. "I don't hold with that nonsense. People should be as generous as they can regardless of the day. When Mr. Singh comes back, he will drive you to see your Gran. Then you are to come back here day after Boxing Day."

Simon frowned, worry creasing his forehead. "Why?"

"You can drive, can't you?"

"Yes, my lady, but I don't see—"

"You're my new chauffeur. I'm tired of Ophelia trying to kill me with her driving."

Simon lost all propriety and nearly smothered Aunt Butty in a hug. How very un-English of him.

Chapter 11

Candles sparkled along the table, each surrounded by a little ring of festive holly. The scents of roast meats and vegetables and savory stuffing teased my nose, so my mouth watered.

It was just the four of us: Aunt Butty, Chaz, Binky, and me. It seemed a bit much—such a large table, groaning with food—for so few of us. Aunt Butty might not hold with Boxing Day tradition, but it was the only way we'd get rid of all this food before it went to waste.

"This will never do," Aunt Butty muttered. "Mr. Singh!"

Mr. Singh appeared, open bottle of red wine in hand. "My lady?"

"Go get Flora and Cook. Are the gardeners and Mr. Phelps about?"

"The gardeners and Mr. Phelps are having Christmas dinner with their respective kin," Mr. Singh said without batting an eyelash. He was used to Aunt Butty's whims. "But I shall fetch the others immediately."

He disappeared, only to reappear a few moments later with Flora and the cook. Flora looked worried. The cook was irritable.

"What's this then?" Cook set her hands on her formidable hips. "Food not up to scratch?" Her tone held a dangerous edge.

"I'm sure it's fine," Aunt Butty said. "Please, all of you, sit."

Cook exchanged glances with Flora, then Mr. Singh. "Wot's that, m'lady?"

"Sit. We're all having Christmas dinner together."

In most houses, the staff eating with the household would be unheard of. But this was Aunt Butty who did things in her own way. Before Cook and Flora knew what was happening, Chaz and Mr. Singh had seated them like proper ladies and taken their own seats.

Binky blinked. "This is highly irregular."

"Oh, pull it out, old man," Chaz ribbed him. "Have a drink."

Before we could enjoy the meal, Flora jumped to her feet and pointed dramatically to the window. "Look!"

We all looked, half expecting to see something ghastly. Instead, there was the Christmas vision of soft-falling snow, blanketing the scenery beyond.

"Well," Aunt Butty said. "It's about time. Happy Christmas, everyone."

I lifted my glass with a grin. All was as it should be.

"Happy Christmas."

Coming in 2019

Lady Rample and Cupid's Kiss

Lady Rample Mysteries - Book Six

Sign up for updates on Lady Rample:

https://www.subscribepage.com/cozymystery

Want more Christmas Cozy Mysteries?

Check out

The Poison in the Pudding,

a *Viola Roberts Cozy Mystery.*

With a book deadline and Christmas fast approaching, the last thing Viola Roberts has time for is a party. Unfortunately, that's exactly what she gets roped into by the Mayor of Astoria. Party planning it is. Complete with Christmas puddings.

Everything is humming along just fine when suddenly the guests begin to drop like flies! With both her reputation and her favorite Christmas cookies threatened, Viola has no time to waste. She's got to find the poisoner before somebody ends up dead.

Note from the Author

Thank you for reading. If you enjoyed this book, I'd appreciate it if you'd help others find it so they can enjoy it too.

- Lend it: This e-book is lending-enabled, so feel free to share it with your friends, readers' groups, and discussion boards.

- Review it: Let other potential readers know what you liked or didn't like about the story.

- Sign Up: Join in on the fun on Shéa's email list: https://www.subscribepage.com/cozymystery

Book updates can be found at www.sheamacleod.com

About Shéa MacLeod

Shéa MacLeod is the author of the bestselling paranormal series, Sunwalker Saga, as well as the award nominated cozy mystery series Viola Roberts Cozy Mysteries. She has dreamed of writing novels since before she could hold a crayon. She totally blames her mother.

She resides in the leafy green hills outside Portland, Oregon where she indulges in her fondness for strong coffee, Ancient Aliens reruns, lemon curd, and dragons. She can usually be found at her desk dreaming of ways to kill people (or vampires). Fictionally speaking, of course.

Other books by Shéa MacLeod

Be Careful What You Wish For

Nothing Tastes As Good

Soulfully Sweet

A Stich in Time

<u>Dragon Wars</u>

Dragon Warrior

Dragon Lord

Dragon Goddess

Green Witch

Dragon Corps

Dragon Mage

Dragon's Angel

Dragon Wars- Three Complete Novels Boxed Set

Dragon Wars 2 – Three Complete Novels Boxed Set

<u>Sunwalker Saga</u>

Kissed by Darkness

Kissed by Fire

Kissed by Smoke

Kissed by Moonlight

Kissed by Ice

Kissed by Blood

Kissed by Destiny